SHAM POO
SHAM POO
Curl Cream
Curl Cream
SHAM POO
SHAM POO
Curl Cream

I Wear Long Hair
Tengo Mi Cabello Largo

Illustrated by Chelsea C. McLin
Cover Design by Chelsea C. McLin
ISBN: 978-1-7378082-0-6 (Hardcover)

AuthorRosaMRomero@gmail.com

Printed by IngramSpark in the United States of America

I wear long hair

This book belongs to

____

This book is for my nephews Aiden, Asher, and Tobias. They inspire me to write books that have story characters that they and other children can relate with.

Hi! I'm Asher and I wear long ***hair*** that makes me feel **Strong, brave** and **different**... but in a good way.

Since I was a baby, my mommy and daddy have let my ***hair*** grow. When I was 2 years old, they wanted to cut my ***hair,*** but I said

My long ***hair*** makes me feel safe and warm on cold winter nights.

My long ***hair*** makes me feel a little bit taller.

My long ***hair*** helps me hide when I am feeling shy.

I *love* the way my mommy runs her fingers through my ***hair*** to help me fall asleep when I am sick.

I *love* the way my grandma pats my ***hair*** when she's proud of me.

I *love* the way my ***hair*** bounces when I run.

One day at school, I noticed that the boys in my class do not have long ***hair*** like me. But the girls do.

Some of the girls wear their ***hair*** in different styles.

This makes me wonder, "Should I have long ***hair?***"

I ask my mommy and daddy, "can boys have long **hair?**" They ask me, "do you like your long **hair?**" I say, "I LOVE my long **hair!**"

They tell me that my long ***hair*** helps me be **strong**, BRAVE and DIFFERENT.

"Different?"
"But I don't want to be DIFFERENT!"

Mommy and Daddy say, "*DIFFERENT* is not a bad thing. We are all *DIFFERENT* in some ways and it makes us who we are." I think about what they say.

On Sundays, it is ***hair*** day. My Tía, comes over and washes, combs, and sprays my ***hair*** with something that will help it stay strong. It feels **funny** when she sprays my ***hair*** and I giggle a little.

Tía braids my ***hair*** and makes me look like a brand new boy. I smile when I see my ***hair*** in the mirror.

I like that my ***hair*** looks different each week. I can wear it in a ponytail or I can wear braids. Or I can wear it out, which is my favorite way to wear it.

When I go back to school the next day, my friends tell me that they *love* my ***hair.*** They say, "It always looks so *nice* and **different**."

I **smile.** I am happy. I feel strong. I feel **brave.** I feel *different…* but in a good way.

I am proud to wear long ***hair.***

About Rosa M. Romero

I Wear Long Hair was inspired by Rosa's handsome nephew, Asher. Asher is Jamaican and Salvadoran American. As a young boy, Asher had long beautiful curly **hair**. He enjoyed showing off his **hair** after his Tía Rosa would braid it. At times, Asher felt shy or sometimes scared! His **hair** helped him feel STRONG, **brave**, and different... but in a good way!

Rosa's parents are from El Salvador and Rosa was born in Washington D.C. She now lives in Greenbelt, Maryland with her dog Bruno. She is an elementary school reading teacher. Her favorite part about teaching is seeing how excited her students get when it is read aloud time! Rosa and her students enjoy discussing what makes a book special. This influenced her to share her student's favorite books on her Instagram @Msromerosbookshelf. She found that her students enjoy reading stories that have characters that look like them and they can relate to. Rosa uses her social media platform to share multicultural and diverse books all children can relate to.

"All children deserve to see story characters that look like them in the books they read." – Rosa M. Romero

SHAM POO
SHAM POO
Curl Cream
Curl Cream
SHAM POO
SHAM POO

CPSIA information can be obtained
at www.ICGtesting.com
Printed in the USA
BVHW021657160922
647245BV00004B/18

9 781737 808206